Little Bunny's Preschool Countdown

Maribeth Boelts

Illustrated by Kathy Parkinson

Albert Whitman & Company • Morton Grove, Illinois

Maribeth Boelts and Kathy Parkinson also worked together on the first book about Little Bunny, titled *Dry Days, Wet Nights*.

Boelts has also written *Grace and Joe* and *Lullaby Babes*.

Parkinson is the illustrator of *Too Much Mush!* She wrote and illustrated *The Enormous Turnip* and *The Farmer in the Dell*.

Library of Congress Cataloging-in-Publication Data

Boelts, Maribeth, 1964-
   Little Bunny's preschool countdown / written by Maribeth Boelts;
illustrated by Kathy Parkinson.
     p.   cm.
Summary: LB spends the summer dreading the first day
of preschool, especially after his second-grade cousin makes
him worry about what it will really be like.
   ISBN 0-8075-4582-1
   [1. Nursery schools—Fiction. 2. Schools—Fiction.
3. Cousins—Fiction. 4. Summer—Fiction. 5. Rabbits—Fiction.]
I. Parkinson, Kathy, ill. II. Title.
PZ7.B635744Li 1996   95-52645
[E]-dc20   CIP
                                       AC

Designed by Lucy Smith.
The text of this book is set in Benguiat Gothic.
The illustrations are rendered in watercolor and ink.

TO MY FAMILY. MB

*

FOR EMILY AND PINK SNAKE! KP

Little Bunny was combing his whiskers in the bathroom when he shouted, "Papa! I can see my eyes now in the bathroom mirror!"

"You're getting taller, LB," Papa said. "Why, before you know it, you'll be four years old. And then, when the summer's over, you get to start preschool."

Later that day, Papa and LB made a calendar.

"Here is today," Papa said. "Then next month, there is the Fourth of July. After July comes August, when we'll have your birthday. And then in September, preschool will begin.

"Every night before you go to bed, you can put an X through the day, and that will help you see how many days there are until preschool begins. Doesn't that sound like fun?"

"Uh-huh," LB said, but he wasn't sure if it really did sound like fun.

LB hung his calendar up by his bed,
and every night after he put on his pajamas,
he put an X through the day.

The garden was growing, and soon it was the Fourth of July. LB, Mama, and Papa brought a blanket and snacks and watched the fireworks in the city park.

"Fireworks are kind of like fancy stars, aren't they?" LB said dreamily.

"That's exactly right," said Mama, pulling LB close.

Cousin Maxine came for a visit. She was going into second grade. She took dancing lessons and knew how to read.

"What's this old thing for?" she asked.

"It's my calendar. I'm putting an X through the days until I go to preschool."

"Preschool...hmmm...," Cousin Maxine said. She looked hard at LB. "Not many days left. You getting scared yet?"

"No...," LB said. "Mama and Papa said it would be fun."

Cousin Maxine twirled in front of the mirror. "Oh, they always say things like that when they want you to do something."

LB's stomach felt worried, but he didn't tell Cousin Maxine. When Aunt Martha and Cousin Maxine left, LB stuck his calendar in the very bottom of his pajama drawer.

HAPPY BIRTHDAY LB!

Soon it was birthday time, and LB was feeling wiggly.
Mama and Papa made a carrot cake with four candles.
When LB finished eating, he opened all his presents.
The last one was from Aunt Martha and Cousin Maxine.
It was a schoolbag with his name stitched on the pocket.

"It's for preschool," Cousin Maxine said, her mouth full
of yellow frosting. "It's coming up *real* soon, isn't it?"

After LB's friends had gone home, and while
his family visited on the porch, LB took his calendar
from his pajama drawer and his new schoolbag, and
he buried them both in the strawberry patch.

The rest of the summer hurried by. LB tried to think about everything except preschool. He rode his bike,

washed Papa's car,

made popsicles
out of lemonade,

and learned how to
write the first letter
in his name.

One hot afternoon, when Mama and LB were weeding the garden, Mama found the calendar and the schoolbag.

"You know, LB," she said gently, "the days keep coming even if you don't mark them with an X on the calendar."

"Oh...," said LB. He thought for a moment. "Mama? It's a very long time until preschool starts, isn't it?"

"No," said Mama. "In fact, preschool begins Monday morning." She took his hand as they carried the strawberries back to the house. "I know it can be scary to try something new, but preschool is a fun place to be. There will be so many things to do, and lots of other bunnies to play with. You'll see."

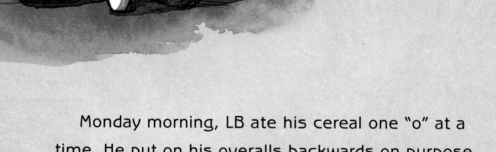

Monday morning, LB ate his cereal one "o" at a time. He put on his overalls backwards on purpose and looked for his shoes in all the wrong places.

As he walked to preschool with Mama and Papa, he kept stopping to look at many interesting things.

"Good morning," said his new
teacher. "I'm so glad that you're coming
to preschool."

LB stood very still and didn't twitch a
whisker while his new teacher and Mama
and Papa talked.

He looked around the room and saw bunnies
painting pictures, building with blocks, and sliding
down a slide. He watched one bunny play with
bright green clay at a table all by himself.

"May I show you where you can hang your schoolbag?" his new teacher asked, holding out her hand.

LB held his bag tighter. "Can I ask Mama and Papa something first?"

"Certainly," said his new teacher.

Mama and Papa bent down low.

LB swallowed hard. "Will you always, always, always come back for me?" he whispered.

"Always," said Mama and Papa, and they hugged LB tight.

LB wiped away just a little tear. As
Mama and Papa waved good-bye, he
took the hand of his new teacher.

"I saw you watching the bunny who is playing with the green clay. His name is Sam. Would you like to join him?" his teacher said.

LB nodded. He sat down at the table and made a row of skinny green snakes, and then Sam made a row of skinny green snakes.

Then Sam smiled.

And so did LB.

And LB thought that even though Cousin
Maxine was going into second grade and knew
how to read and took dancing lessons, she didn't
know everything, especially about preschool.